The Snow King's Daughter

STORY Sowmya Rajendran

PICTURES Proiti Roy

Tulika

"It's so hot!" said Amma, wiping her forehead with the end of her saree.

Keshav looked up from his atlas. He was lying on his stomach on the old straw mat.

"Do you want to go to a cold place, Amma?" he asked, munching the banana chips that his grandmother had given him.

It was vacation time for nine-year-old Keshav and he liked nothing better than looking at his atlas and imagining all the places in the world that he could go to.

Keshav would take his red pencil and put a cross over the names of places he liked. He would roll himself into the old straw mat and pretend he was a grand old man who knew stories about people from these lands. He would make up languages and speak in whispers so that nobody could hear and make fun of him.

Sometimes, when Amma passed by the rolled up mat, she would hear strange hissing noises. But she never guessed that Keshav the Grand Old Man was curled up inside. She only shook her head and said, "You are going to fall sick if you stay inside that mat in this heat!"

"A cold place, Amma! Where there is lots of snow!" said Keshav.

"And where is this cold place with lots of snow?" asked Amma, smiling.

"How about Tibet? The roof of the world,
Amma! So high that our heads will stick into the clouds!"
he exclaimed.

"Silly boy!" laughed Amma. "Do you know that Lobsang is from
Tibet?"

Keshav's eyes widened in surprise.

Lobsang was his neighbour. She lived with her sister and aunt in the
house across the road. Keshav had imagined meeting people from the
names he marked on his atlas many times, but this was the first time he
actually *knew* somebody who was from one of these places.

"Lobsang is from Tibet?" he asked.

"Yes," said Amma. "She came here with her sister when she was a baby."

"Why didn't her parents come?" asked Keshav. He would never dream of going anywhere far away without Amma.

"Her parents are in Tibet, Keshav," said Amma, sadly. "They are not allowed to come to India."

"Why? Then how did Lobsang and her sister come here?" asked Keshav. His mind was suddenly abuzz with questions.

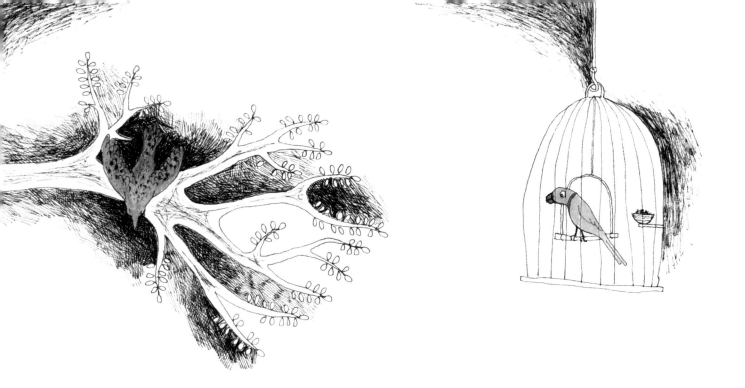

Amma sat down beside Keshav and took the atlas from his hands.

"See," she said, pointing to the map. "This is our country, India. And this is Lobsang's country, Tibet. Now, Tibet is not an independent country like ours..."

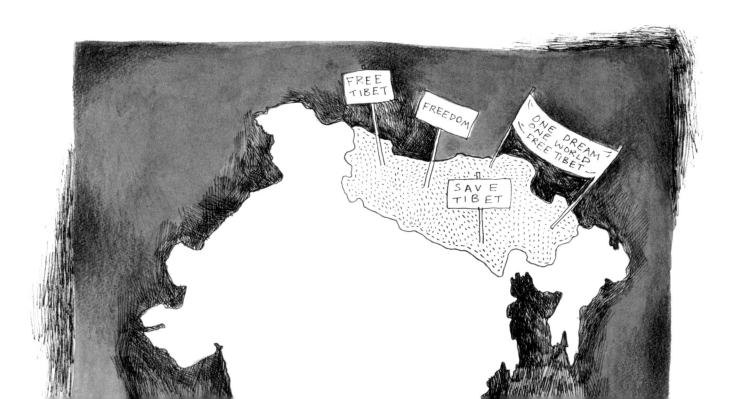

"Why not?" interrupted Keshav. He knew what the word 'independent' meant. He knew that many people had worked hard to make India an independent country.

"Because Tibet is under Chinese rule," said Amma, tapping her finger on the country marked CHINA.

"Then how did Lobsang and her sister come here?" asked Keshav again.

"Their parents sent them with someone who knew the mountains well," said Amma, showing Keshav where the Himalayas stood. "He took them safely across these mountains and they came to our country."

CHINA

HIMALAYAS

INDIA

The Himalayas

"Why didn't they come too?" asked Keshav.
He felt sad thinking about Lobsang's parents
who were so far away in Tibet.

"Because they wanted to stay back and fight for
their land," explained Amma.

Keshav nodded. He understood now.

"Will Lobsang remember all the snow?" he asked.

"I don't know. She was a small baby when she came here. Why don't you ask her?" said Amma, patting Keshav's curly head. Keshav took the atlas back from her and ran out.

"Lobsang!" he called. Lobsang came running out of her house. She was a tiny girl who had lovely brown hair. When she smiled, her crinkly eyes disappeared and all that Keshav could see was the wide toothy grin she gave him always.

"What do you want, Keshav?" she asked loudly. She had a loud voice for such a little person!

"Are you really from Tibet?" asked Keshav excitedly. He still couldn't believe that he knew somebody who was from another place.

"Yes," said Lobsang. "I am from Tibet, didn't you know?"

"No! Tell me, do you remember seeing snow? Real snow?" he asked her.

"Of course!" said Lobsang. "I am the Snow King's daughter. My sister told me that my father will come and take me back to Tibet when they finish building a snow castle for me!" she said shyly.

Keshav smiled. Lobsang did look like a little princess. He plucked
a blade of grass from the ground and said, "Accept this gift from
your humble subject, O Princess of Snow!"

Lobsang laughed and clapped her hands. She took the blade of grass
and said, "I will tell my father, the Snow King, that you are a very
nice boy!"

Keshav bowed low and said, "Thank you, Princess!" He took her
hand and asked if she would like to visit his straw mat house.

"I would love to," said Lobsang, solemnly. She knew that Keshav
never invited *anybody* to his straw mat house. She was very proud
that he had invited her.

They sat inside Keshav's straw mat house looking at the atlas and pretending to be people from places they marked together.

"What is snow *really* like?" asked Keshav.

"It's cold, really cold," said Lobsang, scrunching up her forehead and trying to remember. "And when you let it stay on your hand, it makes little rivers on your fingertips."

"When the Snow King gets angry, does he melt up all the snow?" asked Keshav. He imagined a large man dressed in white robes blowing fire down the snow-covered mountains.

Lobsang giggled. She said, "I think he does! When the Snow King gets really angry, fire comes out of his nostrils and all the snow melts… Then the mountains are easier for our people to cross."

She paused for a moment.

"I hope my father comes soon," she said.

Keshav looked at Lobsang and smiled gently. "I am sure he will," he said. He then put his finger on Sri Lanka which looked like a giant teardrop beneath India and said, "Shall we go here now?"

When Amma went past next, she heard
a lot more hissing noises than usual. But she
didn't understand a word, of course. She only
shook her head and said, "You are going to fall
sick if you stay inside that mat in this heat!"

The Snow King's Daughter (English)

ISBN 978-81-8146-680-8
© *Text* Sowmya Rajendran
© *Illustrations* Proiti Roy
First published in India, 2009

Originally in English

Published by
Tulika Publishers, 13 Prithvi Avenue First Street, Abhiramapuram, Chennai 600 018, India
email tulikabooks@vsnl.com   *website* www.tulikabooks.com

Printed and bound by
Lokavani Southern Printers Pvt. Ltd, 122 Greams Road, Chennai 600 006, India

For more information about Tulika or to order books visit WWW.tulikabooks.com